MINTON

goes DRIVING

ANNA FIENBERG
and
KIM GAMBLE

ALLEN & UNWIN

Minton was thinking about wheels.

'Vroom vroom,' he said, under his breath.

He wanted to make a car *now*.

But he was sitting at a café in the city.

It was his friend Bouncer's favourite place.

'A beetle and banana milkshake, please,' he told the waiter.

'We're fresh out of beetles,' the waiter said sadly. 'How about our special—mango and millipede malt?'

Minton nodded. 'Vroom vroom,' he said to the sugar bowl. '*EEEeeek!*'

'Sssh!' Turtle scowled. 'Do you want to get us thrown out of here?'

'I was doing the screeching tyres bit,' explained Minton.

Minton looked around the café. His car would be yellow—a jaunty jeep maybe? When he'd lived by the sea with Turtle, it had been easy to find what he needed to build things. But where would you start in the city?

As the door to the kitchen swung open, he spied some empty jars in the bin. They had terrific lids.

'Excuse me,' he said to his friends, and tiptoed into the kitchen. 'Is anyone using these fantastic lids?' he asked the cook.

'Nope,' said the cook. 'Go for your life.'

'Is anyone using these old meat skewers?'

'Nope,' said the cook. 'Go for your life.'

'Is anyone using those old butter tubs?'

'Nope,' said the cook. 'But don't eat 'em all at once.'

When Minton got back to the table, he spread his treasure out.

'Bingo!' he cried, rolling four lids across the table. 'Here are my wheels!'

'Uh oh,' sighed Turtle, catching one.

'And here are my axles, see?' Minton held up a skewer.

'What if your car zooms out of control,' said Turtle, 'and goes crashing into a skyscraper and blows up?'

The waiter brought a candle to the table. Outside, the city lights sparkled in a navy sky.

'Ah,' cried Bouncer. 'Good food and good friends. This is the life!'

But Minton was looking at the dead match lying on the napkin. No one would need that. And he might just be able to use it for a handbrake.

Minton hauled his toolbox up onto the table. He took out some scissors and sticky tape.

'Couldn't you at least wait until we've had our earthworm pudding with firefly sauce?' sighed Turtle.

That night, back at the caravan, Turtle yawned
and slipped into bed.

But Minton wanted to work. He began
cutting out the doors for his jeep.

'Will you put out the light now?' said Turtle. 'Some of us around here want to sleep.'

So Minton worked by torchlight. It was a bit hard getting the wheels on while holding the torch.

At midnight, the car was almost finished.

Minton just had to wake Turtle up to
show him.

'I would have painted it white,' Turtle said.
'White cars are easier to see at night. As it is,
enormous trucks and buses will crash into you
for sure.'

Minton went to look for a bumper bar.

At sunrise Minton was ready to go for a test drive. But Turtle was too sleepy. 'Go on, tootle off in your speed machine,' he said, closing his eyes again. 'Look out for walls.'

So Minton skipped off to Bouncer's tent.

'It's a dream machine!' cried Bouncer. 'An ace roadster. A supercharger!'

'Well, I wouldn't go that far,' said Minton. But he looked pleased.

Bouncer did a double somersault and landed in the passenger seat. 'Come on, let's go!'

They headed out into the traffic. Minton roared, 'Vroom vroom!' As they sped down the street Bouncer taught Minton all the road rules, like stopping at the red light and waving politely at the policeman.

The car whizzed along perfectly. It handled the curves, smooth as butter. It hugged the corners like a glove. No enormous trucks or buses crashed into them.

'You're a first class driver, Minton,' said Bouncer.

At morning tea time they stopped at a pirate playground. Bouncer dashed to the swings. Minton ate his sandwiches behind the wheel. 'A car is definitely the best way to get around,' he said dreamily, tooting the horn.

Bouncer and Minton were almost back at the caravan when they came to a huge hill. The car puffed and pooped its way up.

'This is more of a mountain than a hill,'
said Minton.

'Don't worry, we'll make it,' said Bouncer.

At the top Minton smiled. 'A dream machine,'
he said fondly.

Then he gasped. They were flying downhill.
But it wasn't the speed that worried Minton.
It was the wobble.

'My wheel's coming off!' he screamed.

The car swung out all over the road. The
wheel bounced free.

Minton groaned. Now he could see the caravan park. All around it were cars, vans, enormous trucks. He couldn't stop. He couldn't steer.

'Help!' he shrieked.

He looked around wildly. He was going to crash into that postal van. Then he saw something at the bottom. A round hard bump. He was heading straight for it.

'A speed hump!' he cried. *'Bouncerrr!'*

They hit the bump and sailed gracefully over the top, coming to a stop just a bumper bar away from the van.

'I always wanted to be a speed hump,'
sniffed Turtle.

'Or a ski jump,' suggested Bouncer.

Minton put an arm around his neck.
'Thanks, Turtle. Are you all right?'

'I'll live,' said Turtle. 'I suppose.'

After lunch Minton fixed the wheel back on. 'There! Nothing could pull this wheel off. Not even a monster wind. *Now* will you come with me?' he asked Turtle.

They drove to the shops and looked at car radios. At the end of the street was a building site. Minton stopped. He watched an excavator as big as a dinosaur scoop up rocks in its toothy bucket. 'Will you look at that machine!' he gasped.

A loud *beep, beep, beep* filled the air as a gigantic truck backed up towards the excavator.

'Beep, beep, beep,' said Minton to himself softly. He hurried over to the man. 'Excuse me,' he said, 'but I would like to work on this building site. In fact, I can't wait.'

'You'll need a truck then,' said the man, scratching his chin.

'I know,' agreed Minton. 'That's not a problem.'

'Uh oh,' said Turtle. 'No shut-eye again tonight.'

But Minton was already searching for
truck parts. What could he use
to make the dumper?

To make Minton's car you'll need: 2 margarine or butter tubs and a lid, 2 bamboo skewers, 2 corks, 4 plastic lids, glue, tape, paint, and scissors or a sharp knife.

2. Fix steering wheel and base, headlights and bumper with glue

1. Make holes as shown and insert skewers
Cut out doors and seating space as shown

3. Fix hubcap and wheel with glue

15mm

4. Paint the pieces and click together. Clear plastic makes a good windscreen.

Happy driving!